For my two pea pod babies, as different as can be—Jake and Lucy
—K.B.

For Iry and Bobby
—S.W.

Text copyright © 2003 by Karen Baicker
Illustrations copyright © 2003 by Sam Williams
CIP Data is available

"Pea Pod Babies" is a trademark of Karen Baicker and Sam Williams

Published in the United States in 2003 by Handprint Books
413 Sixth Avenue
Brooklyn, New York 11215
www.handprintbooks.com

First Edition
Printed in China
ISBN:1-59354-003-5
2 4 6 8 10 9 7 5 3 1

Pea Pod Babies

Karen Baicker and Sam Williams

HANDPRINT BOOKS 🖐 BROOKLYN, NEW YORK

Once upon a time, a lovely garden bloomed
with rosemary and Queen Anne's lace,
And, of course, a special place
where all the babies grew.

Beyond the bluebells and the beans
hidden deep within the greens,
For those who closely look to see
a magical garden nursery.

And swaying gently in the breeze
there rocked a pod with baby peas.

Tucking them in tenderly
Mama kisses them—
one, two, three.

"Wee baby Sweet Pea,
Sugarplum Snap Pea,
Darling little Snow Pea,
Look at you perfect peas in a pod!"